PALACE
PUPPIES

PALACE PUPPIES

Sunny and the Royal Party

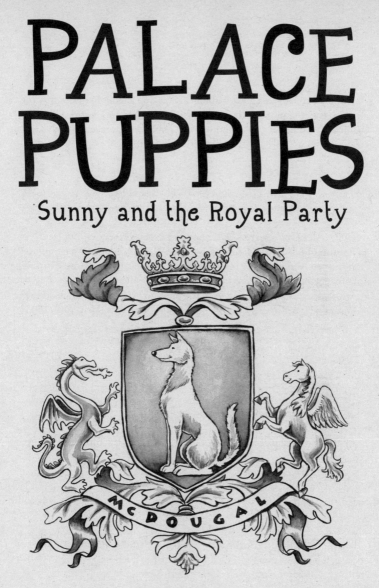

MC DOUGAL

By Laura Dower
Illustrated by John Steven Gurney

𝒟𝒾𝓈𝓃𝑒𝓎 • HYPERION BOOKS
NEW YORK

Printed in the United States of America
First Edition
10 9 8 7 6 5 4 3 2
V475-2873-0 13270

Library of Congress Cataloging-in-Publication Data
Dower, Laura.
 Sunny and the royal party/by Laura Dower; illustrated by John Steven Gurney.—1st ed.
   p. cm.—(Palace puppies)
 Summary: Puppies Sunny and Rex try to save the day when grumpy guest Jackson threatens to ruin the birthday party that the pups' royal owners and best friends, Princess Annie and Prince James, are throwing for him.
 ISBN 978-1-4231-6473-9
[1. Behavior—Fiction. 2. Birthdays—Fiction. 3. Parties—Fiction. 4. Dogs—Fiction. 5. Animals—Infancy—Fiction. 6. Princes—Fiction. 7. Princesses—Fiction.] I. Gurney, John Steven, 1962– ill. II. Title.
 PZ7.D75458Sun 2013
 [Fic]—dc23   2011053518

Visit www.disneyhyperionbooks.com

For CB, Bogie, Olsen,
and all the Labs I've loved

With a shout-out to Jackson,
the real-life O.C. goldendoodle

—L.D.

Chapter 1

Daylight streamed in through the huge floor-to-ceiling windows. I rolled onto my back and looked up through the glass at a wide, blue sky. There was no better view than right here from my doggy bed.

And my belly was so warm.

Out of the corner of one droopy eye, I noticed the tassels on the heavy crimson velvet curtains over my bed. Gold thread glistened in the sun. Of course, *everything* in here glistened: wallpaper, pillows, and rugs.

Even I glistened.

That's because I was the royal goldendoodle.

As I lay there, daydreaming, a door clicked open.

"Rowwrooo?"

I stretched out my legs and quickly rolled back over, my snout nuzzled deep into the pillow. Someone was there, which meant it was probably time to get up. Drat! I didn't want to leave my warm spot! I wanted to get back to the best doggy dream ever. It was the same one I had every night, with wide-open fields, butterflies, and an endless supply of juicy bones. . . .

"Sunny!"

My head popped right up when I heard that voice. Without my even thinking about it, my tail began to stir.

Princess Annie!

Annie came right over, as usual. She was still in her flowered pajamas. Her mane of red curls bounced with each step.

"Good morning, sleepyhead!" she cried.

I expected her to lean down like she always did and pet me. Maybe she'd collapse on the floor and we could snuggle together in the rays of morning sun, with her kissing the top of my head and playfully grabbing my tail. . . .

But I was wrong. Annie didn't even blow me a kiss.

Barking softly, I leaped up and went over to see my princess. Was something the matter? I noticed she wasn't wearing slippers. Aha! This was an opportunity. When Annie had bare feet, I could lick her toes. She would burst into a fit of tickle laughter.

I padded right over and pounced on her feet!

"Not now, Sunny," Annie said, shooing me away.

Hey!

No kisses? No tickles?

Quickly, I got back onto my hind legs and reached up with my front paws. Maybe she'd grab me for a puppy tango. She liked to dance with me that way.

Sometimes, Annie would flick the lights on and off as if her bedroom were some kind of nightclub! She would even dress me up in a pink doggy tutu and pretend I was some kind of ballerina. Annie put me into costumes all the time. It was fun to dress up and dance around with my best friend.

"Woof! Woof! Woof!"

I barked desperately to get Annie's attention. When would we be going for our morning walk? On an ordinary day, we'd have been halfway out the door. Why wasn't the leash in her hand?

Morning walks were the very best part of the days at the palace. Each morning, Annie snapped on my jeweled dog collar and led me outside into the garden. It felt like we walked for miles around the castle property!

Of course, the property wasn't *that* big, but our grand palace did have at least five gardens! I could run or snoop or play fetch-the-stick wherever I wanted. There were loads of smelly smells, and bugs to swat, and cool grass everywhere. . . .

But instead of leading me out the door, this morning Annie rushed around humming to herself. She dashed in and out of her closet carrying armfuls of clothes and shoes—and ignoring me.

"WOOF! WOOF! WOOF!"

I barked as loudly as I could and wiggled my golden body. My tail hit her legs. Annie knew this was puppy code for *Time to go for a walk*. What was the problem?

"WOOOOOOOOOF!"

"Oh, Sunny, you silly dog," Annie said, finally stopping to acknowledge me. "You want to run and play, Sunny, don't you? I know, but I just can't today. James and I have a lot to do this morning!

4

I'll ask Nanny Fran to take you out if you really need to go. . . ."

Nanny Fran?

I plopped down onto the floor. No walk with Annie? That was no way to start today!

James!

I should have known. James was Annie's older brother. His room was all the way at the other end of the long upstairs hall, but he was always hanging out in Annie's room instead.

Why couldn't he just stay in his own room? Or why couldn't he stay in one of the other six bedrooms on this floor of the palace? I wanted to keep Annie all to myself! I wanted my walk!

I still remembered the day I arrived at the royal palace. The king and queen had tied an enormous purple bow around my neck and presented me to my princess wrapped up in a soft purple fleece blanket. Purple was Annie's favorite color (and mine, too)! I was placed upon Annie's pillow. It seemed as if she might roll right over onto me. But of course, Princess Annie was far too gentle to do anything like that!

I didn't remember *everything* about what had happened that day. I was an itty-bitty pup, after all. But since then, I'd seen all the royal photo albums!

Those albums showed that, from the very beginning of my life in the palace, Annie had cared for me as if she were my own mother. There were photos of her kissing my head and shots of her stroking the fur on my ears, paws, and snout. There were even a few videos of me running with her out in the fields behind the palace. I loved to look at those pictures. It made my tail wag just thinking about hanging out with my best friend.

But where Annie was sweet, James always teased me! He made fun of my oversize goldendoodle puppy paws. He chased me around the rooms of the palace until I got lost. He would even act like he was giving me a Snappy Snap snack . . . and then he'd snatch it away.

But now I thought that maybe he had done all that because he was a little jealous of his sister. James had probably just wanted a puppy for his very own! (Well, that and the fact that James thought teasing Annie was his job as her big brother.)

So it was a great day in the palace when James finally got his own pup. James had a constant companion now. And I got a new puppy friend.

The dog was named Rex, after General Randolph Rex McDougal, a family member who had lived in the castle a century ago.

What could have been better than a pair of puppies in the palace?

But it wasn't as perfect as I'd hoped. If Annie and James were different, Rex and I were total opposites.

For starters, Rex was a beagle who was always causing trouble, even if he didn't mean to. I, on the other hand, was a goldendoodle, and I tried to follow the rules.

Rex got overexcited about everything. Trouble seemed to follow him around like a cloud. Just the past week, Rex had decided to run around the palace at top speed. His tail wagged into one of the royal sculptures—a perfect ceramic replica of the castle. It smashed to itty-bitty bits!

But me? I'd never done anything like that. I was a perfect palace pooch. Well, no puppy was perfect. But I liked to try.

Princess Annie's humming snapped me out of my daydream.

She ran from one side of her enormous room

to the other as if she were dashing across the royal tennis court. All that trying on made me dizzy! She would hold up a dressy outfit in front of herself at the mirror and then flip her hair and pose this way and that, then try the outfit on. But every time, she would end up making a face and pulling off the clothes.

Oh, Annie!

Didn't she know she was the prettiest princess in the kingdom? Not that I knew many other princesses to compare with her.

And after all that fussing, she *still* could not decide on an outfit! I watched as she grabbed a beautiful pink lace dress and then a yellow, puffy skirt and then a blue jumper with sparkly thread— all at the same time. Then she threw all three outfits across the room in exasperation.

I wished I spoke human. I would have told her that her white peasant blouse and short purple skirt looked best.

But no one went to the royal dog for fashion advice. (Even though I was always very well groomed.)

I crossed my paws and rested my head on them as I watched her try on a short-sleeved purple sweater, then a blue shirt, and then an orange sundress with a green jacket that had these shiny, silver buttons. . . .

Oooh! Those buttons would be fun to chew on!

All at once, Annie flung the jacket with the buttons right at me.

At *me*!

"Ruff!"

I scrambled out from under it.

What was that for?

I looked up at Annie, but she didn't say a word. The princess was *not* acting like herself today. First, she didn't nuzzle with me, and now she was throwing clothes at me? I didn't like it one bit. I hopped up onto Annie's canopy bed (where I was not usually allowed to jump).

"RUFF!"

I barked and pranced back and forth on the silk coverlet with my messy paws. But did I get her attention? No!

Now, I knew that acting naughty was *not* the way to get Annie's attention. But at that moment, I was willing to try anything. So I took a bite of the green jacket she'd flung at me. I flipped it back and forth like a chew toy. And then I really began to gnaw at those silver buttons. They *were* fun to chew on! They felt cold and hard against my teeth.

Crunch. Crack.

Annie! Did you hear that? I'm wrecking your jacket! Look over here!

But *still* she didn't look at me.

Okay, I thought. This called for some drastic measures. This called for the puppy whimper. It was something I saw Rex do a dozen times a day, and Rex *always* got what he wanted.

I knew I should have been past this whimper-and-whine phase. I was growing out of my puppy ways. But even so, I let out the lowest, saddest puppy whine I could.

"Worororororororrrrrrrrooooo!"

"SUNNY? Is that *you*?" Annie said. She turned to me and immediately spotted her jacket in my mouth.

She marched right over.

"Oh, dear! What have you done to my jacket? There's dog drool all over this! Sunny!" Annie grumbled. "No! Bad dog!"

My ears pushed back. I hated the word *bad*.

I wasn't really a bad puppy, was I? I'd only done

one—okay, two—bad things. And it was only because Annie wasn't paying attention.

Sometimes even a princess could say things that hurt a puppy's feelings.

Annie must have realized that she had hurt me.

"Oh, Sunny," Annie cooed in my ear, "don't look so sad. You aren't really a *bad* dog. I know that. But you need to listen! You can't whimper like that! You can't just do whatever you want. You can't eat my clothes, silly!"

I hung my head.

"Sunny. Look at me. Now, you know I can't stay mad at you, but you need to understand. . . . Today is going to be a long, long day . . . and you need to listen. . . ."

She sounded much sweeter than before. I nuzzled her face with my wet nose.

"I just don't have time right now to give you attention, Sunny," Annie went on. "Right now I need you to stay in the room and keep out of everyone's way. Can you do that? Stay right here? Pretty please?"

I lifted my goldendoodle head and nodded slowly.

I was determined to do exactly what Annie

asked me to do—especially when she said pretty please, because that meant she meant business.

That's the kind of dog I am. I try to do the right thing.

Unlike Rex. Sometimes I think he tries to do everything *but* the right thing.

Rex doesn't realize it when he's doing something wrong. Like, Rex would probably have grabbed Annie's green jacket all over again, thinking it was still time to play, even after everyone in the room screamed, "Stop!" That puppy thinks everything is a game!

Someday, Rex will learn the royal ropes. Until then, however, it's my job as the older palace puppy to help him figure things out.

Annie looked deep into my brown eyes. I blinked. Then I opened my mouth just a little and let my pink tongue roll out, giving Annie my best puppy smile. Wasn't it amazing how pups and princesses just had this special way of understanding each other?

"Annie?" a voice yelled from downstairs. I guessed it was Bill, the butler.

He probably needed the princess to help decorate for the party. His voice was so loud.

"Aaagh! I have so much to do!" Annie threw her hands up in the air. After trying on all of those clothes, her room overflowed with clutter! She tried to put away some of the clothes in the enormous pile, but quickly gave up.

"Aw, I'll just fix this later," she said to me. "I have too many other things to worry about right now."

Then, without another word, she disappeared into the hallway.

I lay down on the bed and did what any good and responsible puppy could have been expected to do. I stayed put. But I felt so restless inside. I liked being busy. I liked running around. And I *really* liked it when Annie was with me, like, for example, when she scratched my back. I liked having her as my best friend! I definitely did not want to stay there without Annie.

What would Rex have done if he were in my dog collar? *He'd have gone and gotten her!*

No puppy let her princess go without a fight! *"Whooooooo!"*

I jumped up onto all fours, ready to leap down and go find Annie. But then I stopped. Annie had said *pretty please.* That meant she really, really needed my help today. She needed me to stay put.

But what if Annie didn't realize that keeping me in the room was a bad idea? What if I was the key to helping her downstairs? And maybe, if I tried really, extra, SUPER hard, I could be an almost perfect pup. I'd be able to help Annie with whatever she needed. James, too!

Annie didn't know it, but I was the very thing she needed this morning. And without another moment's hesitation, I flew off her bed.

Thankfully, the carpet cushioned my reckless leap. Otherwise, I might have dented a paw. Hurriedly I dashed through the bedroom door and out into the long hallway. Was Annie still up here?

She was nowhere to be seen.

Scrambling, I raced to the stairs to find my princess. I barely kept my balance as I made a turn in the hallway and then—

Klonk!

I collided with something. Or, should I say, some *pup*?

"Rex?"

"Sunny!" Rex howled back at me. He whipped around so fast chasing his own tail in a circle that

I wasn't sure what he was doing. "Sunny! Sunny! Sunny!"

"Oh, Rex, get out of my way!" I said.

"Go—down—must—*rrrruff*!" Rex barked.

"Oh, Rex," I grumbled again. "There's no time for puppy games!"

"Down!" Rex barked. "PARTY!"

"Party?" My goldendoodle ears went back.

"Yes! That's what James said," Rex cried. "And I don't actually know what a party is, but he was talking about it all morning. He said there would be lots and lots of treats to eat, and anything with lots and lots of treats to eat sounds good to me!"

Party! So *that* was what all this secret planning was about! That explained why Annie needed the perfect outfit. . . .

My paws began to tap-dance. There was nothing better than a party at the palace! Once Annie threw me a birthday bash on the front lawn and invited all the dogs from the neighborhood for a game of Ultimate Dog Disc Tag! We ran around in the yard until the sun went down, and then all the dogs got their own doggie bags and . . .

Hold on.

My paws stopped doing their party dance.

Why hadn't Annie told me the truth about what they were planning? I had always been included in special palace celebrations till now. So why was I being left out today? Something funny was going on.

Gong! Gong! Gong!

All at once, the grandfather clocks downstairs began to chime. Rex got all worked up again. His tail whipped from side to side like a windshield wiper.

"Rex, would you calm down, *please*?" I said, but he didn't hear me. He just kept wagging and dancing till I was sure he'd knock something over.

Sometimes younger puppies just don't get it.

"Calm down," I said again.

"*Rowrowrowrooooo!*" Rex howled back.

"I said, *shhhhh*!"

I extended my paw to quiet him down.

"Rex, we'll never find out what's happening if you keep howling. First, let's sniff our way downstairs. Once we spot Annie and James, we can figure out what's really going on."

And we can find out why we weren't invited to the party, I thought.

Chapter 2

Rex and I bounded down the grand staircase together.

Well, I bounded. Rex tripped. He said it was a bump in the carpet. That pup is *always* stumbling over his own paws. His mind works faster than his big feet, especially on steps. Luckily for him, he landed back on his paws and not on his snout. If there's one thing I've learned about Rex, it's that he seems to bounce, which is good, since he's a little clumsy.

I took my time, slowly placing one paw in front of the other. Coming down the royal stairs like this made me feel like a queen. All I needed was a scepter and crown.

Ahh: Queen Sunny. I liked the sound of that.

The balustrade (I think that's just a fancy-pants word that means "railing") usually looked dull to me, but today it was polished to perfection. It shone brighter than all the gold at the palace.

Except for *me*, the goldendoodle girl.

"Look!" I barked softly to Rex.

At the foot of the staircase, members of the palace staff rushed to and fro with enormous vases of flowers, trays holding glasses, and bouquets of golden balloons. One of the staff lowered the giant cut-crystal chandelier in the palace entryway. He and another man polished each teardrop-shaped crystal one by one with a soft pink cloth. The teardrops sparkled in the sunlight. They made rainbows along the floor. Rex bounded onto the bright beams, trying to catch a rainbow in his paw. I giggled.

The windows gleamed, and sunlight shone through onto the carpets that stretched across the marble floors. The biggest rug in the room had the family crest woven into the center.

Our family's coat of arms appeared all over the palace: etched into the glassware, included in the wallpaper pattern, and even painted on the drawing room ceiling. It's a very old crest that dates back to the fourteen hundreds. That's, like, a zillion years ago. The coat of arms shows a dragon on one side, a horse with wings on the other, and a very regal-looking dog at the center. At the top is a crown just like the one the king wears on special occasions at the palace.

The best thing about the palace coat of arms was that it was always painted or woven in gold.

Just like me!

One Christmas, the family had a doggy sweater made especially for me—with the crest knitted in purple and gold yarn. Wearing that crest meant I was as royal as any pup out there!

But most importantly, wearing that coat of arms meant I was part of a royal family. I was special.

My tail wagged at that thought.

No sooner had we scurried away from the bottom steps than a side door opened and Annie appeared. I wanted to rush over and jump into her arms. But that was impossible. She was carrying an enormous box overflowing with colored plastic objects. What was inside that box? Toys? Games? Presents?

What kind of a party was this going to be? We needed to find out fast if we were going to help Annie and James.

"Get back!" Rex warned me. "If Annie and James see us, they'll send us back upstairs!"

"Did James tell you to stay upstairs, too?" I asked.

Rex panted, "Yeah!"

I could understand why they wanted Rex to stay upstairs, but what about me? Didn't they know what a big help I was?

We really had to find a better, safer hiding place. This was getting risky.

Quickly we scrambled toward the other side of the room. The two of us crouched together behind one of the giant chairs there. I loved how the chair's red velvet cushions felt *so* soft when I rubbed my ears against them.

I hated sneaking around, but now Rex and I were in this together. I knew that Annie had already asked me—*twice*—to stay put. Even though I was the wiser and older puppy, I'd broken the rules; I just wanted to help my princess! I was as excited as Rex was about the idea of a party, and I really hadn't meant to upset Annie.

I knew what happened when Annie got upset. She wouldn't leave me alone anymore. She'd ask Nanny Fran to watch me!

Nanny Fran!

All that woman did was hold me way too tight and treat me like I was a little baby. What if Annie put Rex with Nanny Fran, too? I would have to spend an entire afternoon stuck in a room with that beagle. Nanny Fran would probably dress us up in matching outfits.

For example, the matching baby rompers with lace and snaps, and the cowgirl dress with fringe, accompanied by the

black-and-white cow costume for dogs. And what about the matching luau shirts with hula skirts?

Bleccch!

"*Psst!* Sunny?" Rex whispered to me as we hid behind the chair. "I know this sounds crazy, but . . . what exactly *happens* at a party?"

"You don't know?" I chuckled.

Rex's ears went back, which meant he was a little embarrassed.

"I've only tasted party cake once, and that was up in James's room, after one of the king's parties. I never actually saw a real palace party while it was happening."

My doggy jaw dropped. There were always so many parties in the palace that I couldn't believe Rex had never seen one. But sometimes I forgot how new Rex was to the family. He had been adopted by James only a short time before.

I needed to remember this stuff. Being understanding and patient was what being a big sister was all about.

"The first thing you should know, Rex," I explained, "is that a party is a celebration, a happy time."

"Happy?" Rex panted. "Happy! Happy! Happy! Whoops!"

His tail started wagging so fast he nearly pushed himself forward from behind the chair. For a split second, I was afraid someone might have seen us.

"Control yourself," I said.

"But I was just feeling *happy*. . . ."

"A puppy can get tossed out of a party for acting *that* happy."

Rex and I giggled together.

"What else is at a party?" Rex asked. "Is there food?"

"*Food?*" I exclaimed. "That's the best part. During the party, a puppy's job is to roam in and out of the rooms looking for people food."

"How?" Rex asked.

"First, find a spot to sit in near the buffet table. Guests serve themselves on these huge spoons. Half of the food drops onto the floor! The staff passes around tiny pieces of food on a tray, and a lot of that drops, too."

Once I was crouched down in the corner of the room when someone dropped *an entire chicken leg*. I swooped over and grabbed it in my teeth. Then I dragged it behind the sofa before anyone knew what had happened.

"You need to perfect your puppy-dog face," I explained.

"Oh," Rex woofed, "I'm good at that one." He frowned a teeny bit. He whimpered, too, perfectly.

"Remember, Rex, that no matter what, you must stay alert at all times. Make sure no party guests trip over you. That would make Annie and James very unhappy. Trust me."

"Did that ever happen to you?" Rex asked.

I nodded and covered my eyes with one paw. "One time," I said slowly, "I tripped the queen."

"No way!" Rex blurted out.

"Yes, but thankfully, she made a speedy recovery," I said. "She only broke the heel on her royal sandals, and stumbled in the courtyard."

"Gee, Sunny, you're so smart; you know how to make everything better," Rex said.

"Not *everything*," I smiled. "But thank you."

"Is there dancing at the party?" Rex asked. He began turning in fast circles again. "James was practicing some moves in his room."

"Yup, there's plenty of dancing," I replied, doing a little puppy jig of my own. "Annie likes to dance, too."

Rex started to show me his best dance moves. It didn't take much to get this pup all revved up!

He wagged and wiggled all over the place.

"Party!" Rex cheered. "I love to dance!"

"*Shhhhh!*" I said, lowering my voice to a whisper. "Listen. I saved the most important thing you need to know for last: important party rules of *behavior* for puppies."

"Aw," Rex growled, "I hate behaving!"

"Well, palace puppies are expected to behave at all times. If you act up, you'll get dragged out of the party by both paws and get sent straight to Nanny Fran. Got it?"

"Oh, no," Rex said.

"So that means no whimpering," I explained. "No bumping. No jumping. No nuzzling. No feet licking. No barking. No stalking. Got it?"

Rex didn't get it. He was staring at a fly that had landed on the velvet chair. He swatted at the fly.

"*Got it?*" I asked again.

"Um . . . what . . . huh?" Rex asked, swatting again at the fly.

I rolled my eyes.

"Hey, will there be other dogs at the party?" Rex asked.

"Maybe. Sometimes human guests bring their puppies."

"Seems like a waste of time to bring a puppy when we aren't allowed to bark or have any fun," Rex grumbled.

"We make our own fun," I said.

Just then I heard a loud clang. Annie was back.

Rex and I quickly pressed our little doggy bodies up against the chair. We held our breath until she passed. A group of palace staff people came by after that with armloads of folding chairs, tables, and crates that clinked with glasses and bottles in all shapes and sizes.

I stuck my nose in the air. There was an unfamiliar smell here, as well. What was it?

Rex sniffed, too.

"Hey." Rex nudged me. "I'm getting kind of hungry. Maybe we can stake out a spot near one of those tables with the big silver trays on them?"

"I don't know," I said. "Annie might see us."

"Nah," Rex insisted. "Let's just go. Come on!"

The truth was it *was* downright squishy behind this chair. But I also didn't want to get caught—and sent back to the room. Just the thought of Nanny Fran dressing me in doggy diapers made my fur stand on end. . . .

"Hey, do you smell that? I smell something good!" Rex yelped.

A scent filled the air with sweetness, like pancakes. But it wasn't pancakes.

"There is only one way to correctly ID that scent." Rex licked his chops. "We must investigate."

And just like that, Rex took off into the corridor.

"Hey!" I called after him.

I knew I shouldn't go. I was afraid of disappointing Annie any more than I already had. She took such good care of me. I couldn't let her down—especially on a party day like today.

But I also knew I had to look out for Rex.

He had taken off like a jet plane!

There was no time to waste.

I wished he operated at speeds other than fast and faster and faster than that. . . .

I raced down the hall to find him, my tongue flapping all the way.

Chapter 3

Where had that puppy gone? I raced from room to room looking for Rex. All at once, he leaped in front of me and wrestled me to the carpet.

"Food!" Rex cried, sniffing wildly at the air.

I took a deep breath. The air smelled like the perfect mix of flowers and sugar and . . . bacon?

I knew we probably shouldn't be following our noses through the hallway, but the smells were *so* good. Like breakfast. I *loved* breakfast.

Rex spotted a twisted curtain behind a table. He barked at it, as if to say, *Let's check this out!*

There was a hidden door there, with an old glass knob.

Where did the door lead to? Had we found a secret room?

Long ago, the palace had been transformed from a very old and creaky stone fortress into a modern castle. But there were still so many secret passageways! Last spring I'd found a mystery door at the back of Annie's closet, but that had been locked.

Finding this secret route to the kitchen made me feel like a puppy superspy. There were hundreds of places to hide in—and loads of places to discover.

We slid behind the table in the hall. Without much effort, we pushed our puppy bodies up to the door. It opened and revealed a strange gap in the wall that led to a long tunnel. We sneaked inside. Wow! I wasn't even afraid: this was too exciting. At the end of the tunnel were two bolted doors. But the locks were rusted open. This was our lucky day! One door was marked ICE. The other door was marked GRAIN. I didn't know what that word meant, so I went up for a closer sniff.

It smelled like burning firewood! Mmmmm! Now I knew for sure we were a bone's throw away from the kitchen's open hearth. We'd found our palace kitchen!

Hopefully, we had also found the food we'd been smelling for the last half hour.

Rex entered first.

"CA-A-A-A-A-A-AKE!" Rex shouted as soon as he went in. There, on one table in the center of the kitchen, sat a monster-size, many-layered cake. It was probably as tall as me.

Frosted on it in blue were these letters: HAPPY BIRTHDAY JA.

I'd seen palace cake plenty of times, but never any this *big*.

Just *looking* at this cake made me drool a puddle onto the floor.

"Who is this for?" I said, thinking aloud. "Is *JA* for James?" I couldn't read many words, but I definitely knew how to spell *Annie* and *James*.

"*JA* can't be on a birthday cake for James," Rex said. "James's birthday is in the fall, and it's still spring!"

"Um . . ." I tilted my head to one side. "Then who is it for?"

Rex's nose sniffed at the air. "It smells so-o-o-o good. . . ."

We walked closer and closer until the smell of vanilla was all around us. I felt as if I'd been baked into the middle of the cake. My puppy tummy rumbled like the palace bowling alley.

"You keep watch and I'll dive onto the counter," Rex instructed me.

Before I could respond, Rex took off. He aimed his snout for the countertop and propelled his little beagle legs up, up, UP!

But Rex couldn't reach it.

"Aw!" Rex turned back to me. "You do it," he said.

"That cake doesn't belong to us," I said, sounding more like Annie than like myself. "It belongs to JA."

"We don't even know who that is!" Rex said.

I shrugged. "Well . . ."

"Sunny, isn't this a party?"

"Yes. So?"

"You said parties are all about being happy, right?"

"Right."

"Well, *that* cake will make me very happy!" Rex barked.

I hated to admit it, but Rex was right. Just looking at the cake and smelling it was making me pretty happy, too.

All at once, I began to dream up different ways of getting the cake: a supersize cake net, or maybe a cake magnet, or what if I could just find a pair of spring-loaded paws to jump up with?

I squinted.

That cake *could* have been mistaken for a humongous dog treat if I looked at it just so. And we deserved cake for being good royal dogs, right?

My stomach was aching so much by now that I would have told myself *anything* to justify attacking that cake plate.

Rex just egged me on.

"Go on! Get the cake! It's easy to reach!" he cried. "Just take one leap onto the stool, and then the counter, and then lean forward and take a big, big bite. . . ."

Sure, I thought, easy for you to say. You dream about this kind of stuff all the time.

But this was new territory for me.

Here I was, acting like a foolish puppy all over again. But I *had* to do this.

Jump! My claws scraped the metal sides of the table. Oh, no! I started to fall forward, but with one big final push, I made it onto the stool!

Whew.

I glanced down at Rex on the floor. His eyes weren't on the stool or on me. His eyes were on the cake.

Okay, I told myself, *you can do this. Just count to five and fly into the frosting.*

"Ruff! Ruff! Ruff!" Rex called out. That was doggy for *Leap! Leap! Leap!*

His little face looked so happy down there. The truth was that I felt happy, too. Well, happy and nervous at the same time. I took a deep breath.

But just as I was about to launch myself onto the counter—

"SUNNY!" someone yelled. "WHAT DO YOU THINK YOU ARE DOING?"

Annie?

I turned quickly and saw that it was my princess, with her hands on her hips, glaring at me. Then I lost my balance. My claws scratched madly at the stool, but I couldn't hang on. I plunged to the kitchen floor.

Crash!

Rex thought my landing was fantastic. He spun around next to me, chasing his tail. "So close! So close!" he cried.

I was so embarrassed.

How had I let Rex talk me into this mess? Now I'd ruined my chances of getting a party invitation, all because of a silly piece of cake. I knew better. And all I wanted to do was help Annie. I felt so ashamed that I had almost let a cake ruin that.

"OUT OF THE KITCHEN!" Annie cried. "One more naughty move and I'm calling someone to watch over you two!"

Nanny Fran.

Rex and I scooted out of the kitchen and back into the palace entry hall.

Annie didn't chase us—at first. She was probably checking for paw prints in the cake frosting. Rex and I scampered away. We would have to face up later to what we'd done. But for now, we just needed to *hide!*

I saw members of the palace staff headed into the ballroom. Butlers and maids moved all around us. Annie was nowhere to be seen. But Rex spotted James on a ladder. He was hanging colorful streamers on the wall.

The whole ballroom was decorated in a special theme. It seemed to be Royal Birthday Circus. Everything was bright and fun.

"Sunny!"

Annie's voice boomed behind us. She *was* here, after all.

"What were you two doing in the kitchen?" Annie yelled. "James, I found these two trying to steal the cake!"

Rex didn't seem to care that he'd been caught red-handed in the kitchen. He danced over to James, wagging his tail, as if *nothing* had happened.

But I, unlike Rex, cared a lot about what had happened. I bowed my head so low that my ears dragged on the floor. Would Annie ever forgive me?

"Sunny, I'm so disappointed! Why would you do that?" Annie scolded me. "And after I asked you to stay upstairs!"

I knew that what I had done was wrong. But once I got a glimpse and a sniff of that cake—I had to go after it! No puppy on the planet would have passed up that chance.

Annie stroked the top of my fuzzy yellow head as if she understood what I was thinking. I leaned into her hand. All morning I had tried to get her attention. *I finally had it.*

Unfortunately, I'd been a bad dog in getting it,

so it didn't feel as good as it usually did to have her pet me now.

"*Wooooorf!*"

That was my barked apology.

"Sunny, what's going on with you? I know you feel left out today. And I don't mean to ignore you, but I told you that we're busy. . . ."

I nuzzled her knee.

"Hey, Sunny, that tickles!" Annie threw her arms around me. I could feel her heart beating.

"Maybe we should let the dogs help set up for the party after all?" James suggested.

"Really?" Annie huffed. "They'll just make a mess, James."

I looked up at her with my widest puppy-dog eyes. *I won't make a mess,* I tried to say. *I can't speak for the loudmouthed beagle over there, but I'm the best pup in the palace. You know that!*

Annie just smiled. "What am I going to do with you, puppy dog?"

On the other side of the room, James gave Rex his own back-scratching. But Rex never apologized! That puppy just didn't understand how to behave.

James opened a jar marked TREATS.

"Hold it!" Annie said. "You're going to give Rex a treat after he and Sunny almost destroyed our party cake?"

"Come on, sis. It's one lousy beef stick. A chewy snack will keep the dogs busy. Our party guests are going to show up in an hour."

Annie threw her hands up in the air. "Fine," she said.

James tossed rawhide sticks to each of us. I could play fetch all day long with the beef-flavored ones.

"You didn't forget about Jackson, did you?" Annie asked her brother. "He's coming early today, remember?"

"Whoops," James said. "I *totally* forgot."

I looked up from my rawhide chew.

Jackson. I knew that name. J-A-C-K-S-O-N. That started with a *JA*, just like on the cake! Hold on! Was that Jackson's cake in the kitchen? Someone must have stopped frosting before adding all the letters in his name.

Jackson was a first cousin of Annie and James. He lived far, far away, but whenever he visited, he acted like he owned the place. He was the older cousin, but I remembered that he threw tantrums like a real baby. He always wanted to have his way.

"Why do we always have to play with Jackson when he visits?" Annie sighed.

"Because Mom and Dad say so," James said. "And they are the queen and king. That's why."

In all the palace photos, Annie was smiling, and James was smiling, but Jackson was always frowning. I always wondered why.

"It's almost time to take the dogs for a walk before the party, too," Annie said to her brother.

I perked right up when I heard that. Walk? Yay!

"Tell me again why we don't have a royal dog walker?" James asked.

"Because," Annie said, "Sunny and Rex are our puppies, remember? Mom gets angry whenever I ask Nanny Fran to walk them. We're supposed to be responsible for our own pets."

"Well, it stinks," James said.

Rex glared at his prince. "It stinks?" he whispered to me. "I thought he and Annie *loved* walking us! Hmmph!"

"We love walking our dogs!" Annie declared loudly as she clipped on our royal jeweled collars and leashes. She said that as if she'd read Rex's thoughts. Sometimes I believed she could.

"I know, I know. I do love walking Rex," James said. "Just, sometimes, when I have homework and all these chores to do—"

"James, when was the last time you did chores?" Annie cracked. "Look, Mom told us a million times that having a puppy is a huge responsibility. But it's also really, really fun! Let's go."

The four of us walked through a set of French doors. Our collars jingled all the way.

Any time we go outside of the castle, even onto the palace grounds, we have to wear tags that say who we belong to. For example, mine says: SUNNY, THE ROYAL DOODLE. MCDOUGAL PALACE.

Of course, I would have preferred *not* wearing a collar around my golden neck, even one with my name on it. But I didn't want to complain.

The doors led out to one of the palace's sixteen stone patios. Stones from the garden had been placed in a twisting ivy pattern. I loved the way those smooth stones felt on the bottoms of my paws. Some rocks could be rough, like the ones at the seashore.

I loved this garden! The air smelled so fresh and wet. The sky was different shades of blue.

"Hello-o-o, Charlie!" Annie called out to the palace gardener.

Charlie stood on a wooden ladder, doing last-minute snips on some of the topiary with a huge pair of shears. He trimmed a few leaves here and a few more there. This gardener could turn an ordinary old bush into a skyscraper or an animal!

All along one fence, Charlie had trimmed a row of topiary into the shapes of different dog breeds. After all, no puppy palace was complete without its puppy topiary. One of the clipped bushes actually looked a lot like me. It had golden leaves on top, just like my goldendoodle head.

There were bushes in other dog shapes and sizes, too: poodles, greyhounds, huskies, sheepdogs, and more. Nearby, I spotted a beagle-shaped topiary with cute, floppy ears.

That one looked exactly like Rex!

I couldn't get enough of the trees, the gravel, everything. I chewed whatever I could find: a pinecone, some grass, and half of an apple that someone (probably Charlie the gardener) had tossed away.

Mmmmm. I loved tart apples.

After a little time had passed, Rex tackled me

and we started to wrestle in the grass. It was much easier to play out here. We didn't have to worry about breaking anything. Rex kept lifting his head up high in the air, sniffing around. There were so many sounds and sights. Rex got distracted easily.

Wind! Dragonfly! Grass! Cloud! Sunny!

Annie and James had sat on a bench, but they kept getting up and looking back toward the palace. I could tell they were very excited about the start of the party. I know that it's hard to sit still when you're excited!

Then, out of nowhere, we heard a loud, strange noise: *NOOOOOOOOOOOOOOOOOO!*

It sounded like someone was upset. My paws started to twitch.

Annie leaped right off the bench. "Oh, no! What was *that*?" she asked.

"I have a feeling I know," James said. "But we should go back inside and find out for sure."

Chapter 4

"Sunny! Rex! Hurry!" Annie cried, scurrying into the palace ahead of us. She snapped off our collars and leashes when we were inside.

We headed for the source of the noise.

"Jackson!" James said as soon as he saw his cousin. "I guessed it was you."

Jackson just grunted. "Yeah, it was me."

"Is something the matter?" Annie asked him.

Jackson stuck out his tongue. "I thought you'd be here to greet me."

"We were walking the dogs," Annie explained. "But we're back now! Welcome to your party!"

"Yeah," Jackson grumbled. "Some welcoming committee."

Now I knew why Annie had worked extra hard to make this party so special. She wanted to make sure grumpy old Jackson got a smile on his face! My princess was so thoughtful.

Too bad Jackson wasn't.

I also understood now why Annie and James had hidden us dogs away that morning! They didn't want us underfoot, and they didn't want Jackson to freak out when he saw the two of us. Last year, Jackson had demanded that I be put out of the castle so he would not get dog hair on his party suit.

When Rex trotted over to bark a loud hello, Jackson jumped back.

"Get away from me, you . . . dog!" he gasped. He swatted at Rex like he was some kind of bug. "Get him away, James! Now!"

James picked Rex up and shook his head. "Aw, Jackson, he won't hurt you," he said. "Rex is a royal beagle."

Jackson made a face. "I don't like dogs. You know that."

"Nice outfit," Annie said, changing the subject. She complimented her cousin on his birthday pants and shirt.

Jackson wore a bow tie with little polka dots printed on it. He always dressed up. "Why aren't *you* dressed up for my party, Annie?" he asked.

"Oh! I have a dress all picked out! We were going to head upstairs to change as soon as we finished walking the dogs," Annie replied. "We've been so busy setting up the party all morning we lost track of time."

"I thought the palace staff was in charge of all the preparations," Jackson said.

"No, we're in charge," James said. "The royal magician is coming later this afternoon."

"But I wanted a court jester," Jackson said.

"Well, we have jugglers!" Annie added cheerily.

"Yawn," Jackson said, covering his mouth with one hand.

"And acrobats, too," Annie added.

Jackson shrugged.

And a great big wonderful cake! I wanted to bark.

"Everyone is coming, and we have loads of activities planned!" Annie said. "I organized all the party games. James planned all the music."

"But I hate games," Jackson said. "And I hate music."

"No you don't," Annie said, smiling. "Come on!"

"Nobody hates *games*!" James said.

Rex growled.

"And I hate dogs most of all!" Jackson said, shooting him a look.

I got down on all four paws, ready to pounce. How dared Jackson speak to Annie and James that way? Annie was trying her best to make Jackson feel comfortable, but all he knew how to do was complain.

"There's something missing," Jackson said. He looked around the room. "Where are all my presents?"

"Oh," Annie said, "well, since none of the guests have arrived, there are no gifts yet."

"What about *your* presents for me?" Jackson asked.

"Our presents?" James muttered. "Seriously? Uh . . ."

Jackson crossed his arms. "It *is* my party. I'm allowed to ask for what I want."

Rex growled a little again. What was Jackson going to say now?

"Why is the party inside on such a sunny day?" Jackson whined.

Sunny! I thought. Like me! That was a good thing, right?

Of course, he didn't mean it to be a good thing. He did nothing but complain.

"I asked to have my party outside," Jackson groaned.

Annie looked confused. "Wait. Wasn't it your idea to have it inside?" she asked.

"N—no . . ." Jackson stammered.

"It *was* your idea!" James said.

Rex started growling again.

"*Shhhhh!*" I nudged Rex. "Quiet. You don't want to get James and Annie into trouble, do you? We'd better stay out of it."

"Trouble? Jackson is the troublemaker," Rex said.

"Takes one to know one, eh?" I sniped.

Rex shot me a look. "Very funny, Sunny."

I grinned. "Thank you."

"Look, cuz," Annie explained, "we've already set up the tables and the ballroom games, and . . . we can't really move the party. It's too late. But I know you'll love it."

"Then I demand to see the main room for the party—now!" Jackson insisted.

"Don't you want to be surprised later?" James asked.

Jackson sighed. "What do *you* think? I hate surprises."

"Can you hang out just a little while longer while we go upstairs and get dressed up?" Annie asked.

"You want me to wait around for my own birthday party?" Jackson gasped, exasperated.

"I'm sorry," Annie said. She elbowed James.

"Yeah, we're sorry," James added.

"Well, if I have to wait, I'm *not* waiting here. I'm going for a walk!" Jackson yelled. "Come and find me when you're ready! And if everything isn't perfect, I'm—I'm leaving!"

And just like that, he turned on his heel and left the ballroom.

"Oh, no!" Annie's face fell. "Jackson's leaving? What are we supposed to do now? After all our hard work!"

"Don't stress out, sis. Let's go tell Mom and Dad what's going on," James said. "We'll tell them he isn't happy. They'll know what to do next."

"I don't want the very first party we're in charge of to be a flop!" Annie declared. "Mom and Dad will be so disappointed. And even though Jackson can be . . ."

"A brat?" James said.

Rex and I nodded.

"—Um, difficult," Annie continued, "he is our cousin and he deserves to have a good birthday."

I went over and nudged Annie with my snout as if to say, *It won't be a flop! It's fantastic!*

But she waved me away. "Sunny, take Rex and go back to my room," she pleaded. "We want you two out of Jackson's way—and out of trouble—for real this time. Got it? No funny business!"

I nodded my goldendoodle head. It was time for this royal puppy to be royally loyal. One thing about goldendoodles was that we always tried to see the sunny side of every situation, no matter what.

Rex didn't want to leave, but after a few seconds he started up the stairs with me. Halfway up, he stopped and turned.

"Now what?" I asked.

"I can't do it," Rex said.

"Can't do *what?*" I asked.

"I know we promised to go upstairs, but I can't. Just like I can't let Jackson wander around our palace and ruin everything. We have to keep an eye on him!"

"Rex! We can't follow the guest of honor all around the palace!" I barked.

"Why not? This is *our* palace," Rex said. "We're just doing the right thing for our family."

"Jackson *is* family, remember? He's Annie's cousin," I said.

"He may be a royal cousin," Rex said, "but he's still a royal pain. And I won't let him spoil the party that Annie and James have planned."

"So what are we supposed to do, Rex?" I asked. "We don't even know where Jackson went!"

"Rwwwfff!" Rex answered. He pointed one paw toward the stairs.

"Downstairs?" I exclaimed. "We can't break our promise. We have to stay put."

"But we can't help from up there," Rex whispered. "Let's find other cool passageways. Let's sniff him out! Annie and James won't even know, if we stay well hidden."

He had a point. After all, it was our job to help our best friends.

"We *have* to be extra careful," I said. "Extra, *extra*."

Even if I'd said *no* to his idea, Rex would have gone back down. So it was better for me to go with him.

That way I could keep an eye on Jackson and Rex at the same time.

We did the doggy dash back down the staircase and disappeared into a hall closet. From there, we had a view of two hallways, the kitchen door, the ballroom entryway, and a few rooms, too. It was a perfect place to start.

Rex pushed the door open just a smidge, just enough to let in a sliver of light and a teeny bit of air.

"What now?" I asked after we'd sat there a moment.

"We wait for Jackson to pass by," Rex said. "And then we get to work!"

I started scratching under one ear. I do that when I get nervous.

Rex put his paw on top of mine. "Don't worry so much!" he said. "You're Superpuppy, remember? You do everything right."

I just looked at him, dumbfounded.

As nervous as I felt, I wondered if, maybe for the first time, Rex appreciated me.

And it felt great to be the older, wiser pup-in-charge.

Now if I could have just stopped scratching my ear, things would have been perfect.

Chapter 5

We had to wait only a few short minutes before Jackson reappeared. He stopped right in front of the door we were hiding behind.

I was sure he'd hear us and find us in that closet, but just as he was opening the door, there was a loud clatter, and he took off down the hall.

"What was that?" I asked Rex.

"Dishes?" Rex said, panting.

"KITCHEN!" we both cried at the same time.

We poked our noses out. Where was Jackson headed *now*? He was looking for something. He jiggled doorknobs and stuck his head into rooms up and down the hallway. He was so nosy!

But Jackson still looked unhappy. I wanted to

rush up to him and lick his toes or tickle his nose with my fur. He needed to smile! After all, it was his birthday.

When it had been my birthday in the palace, I felt like the most special puppy in the world. I walked around proudly with my snout in the air.

And Annie had showered me with love—and dog bones.

We saw Jackson sneak down a short staircase. I knew where that led: to the game room and bowling alley.

"*Shhhh!* We need to be quiet," I warned Rex.

I knew the floors in there weren't carpeted, so Jackson would probably hear the click-clack of our claws behind him. Rex and I had to keep as quiet as possible. We did not want to be identified.

Of course, that was easier said than done. Rex's middle name should have been Noisy.

Clickity-clackity, clickity-clackity.

Thanks to Rex, Jackson definitely heard our doggy nails moving across the floor. "Who's there?" he asked, whipping around. Lucky for us, there were wide benches nearby. We darted behind them.

"I said, *who's there?*" Jackson bellowed again.

His loud voice echoed in the royal bowling alley.

When he didn't get an answer, Jackson walked over and grabbed a bowling ball. He threw it down the alley. He was mad.

The ball went into the gutter. That made him madder. Jackson threw another bowling ball, and another, until all the pins at the end had been knocked down. The sound of the bowling balls drowned out the noise of our paws and claws as we sneaked closer to spy on him.

Rex found another place for us to hide, between two racks of bowling balls. But just as we got resettled, Jackson stormed out of the alley.

"Hey! Where is he going now?" Rex whined.

"Shhhhh!"

We scooted out and chased after Jackson again. He walked for a while, not stopping. Then he made his way to the palace gallery. This was a long hallway decorated with portraits and photographs of royal family members. I had visited there before, with Annie. Rex had never seen it, not even just passing through.

New places meant a whole bunch of new smells to capture a pup's attention. Inside potted plants, on the carpet, everywhere, were things to sniff. I had to make sure Rex kept his focus. We had to stay out of sight. I wasn't sure how Jackson would react if he knew that two dogs—dogs he *hated*—were following him.

I loved this gallery! It was one of the best spots in the palace. There were row after row of portraits, and they all stared back at me as if they had a deep, dark secret. Some paintings showed family members from hundreds of years ago. A few of them even looked like Annie and James!

I wondered what the palace had been like way back then.

Up ahead, Jackson stopped at almost every picture. I thought maybe he was saying something when he stopped. Rex and I sneaked a little bit closer to listen.

"Hey, old guy!"

Jackson was talking—to one of the portraits.

"Tell me. What did the palace do for you for your birthday?"

The old guy in the picture had a long gray beard and wore a dark suit and spectacles, which is the old-fashioned word for *glasses*.

"Did they leave you alone instead of asking you to play a game?" Jackson asked the painting.

Of course, the picture didn't answer him, so Jackson moved along to the next one.

The next portrait showed a girl in a long, flowing dress. Her hair was decorated with flowers. Jackson grinned when he saw her.

"I bet you got all the presents you wanted on your birthday, didn't you?" Jackson muttered to the girl. "I bet everyone actually *liked* you, didn't they?"

I turned to see if Rex had heard that, too. He was too busy sniffing a leather chair. I listened closer.

Then, Jackson stopped short in front of a painting of a man dressed in a blue army uniform. This man looked older than the other old guy.

Jackson stood eye to eye with the portrait. I thought he was going to poke his finger through it.

"What are you looking at?" Jackson said to the picture. "Not much, right?" he said, answering his own question.

Why would he say that?

All at once, Jackson spun around. I thought he was going to see us, so I scrambled behind a potted fern.

Rex scrambled after me.

"You're no better than my real party guests!" Jackson said to the row of paintings. "Are you?"

Now, many of the paintings here were very old, but other paintings were new. There was a portrait of Jackson and his family. In it, he was dressed in his best suit, but he was, as usual, frowning.

"I wish you had a brother or a sister," Jackson said to the painting of himself. "Or a real friend."

I pricked up my soft ears when I heard that.

I *really* wished I could have jumped up on Jackson and told him not to worry. I bet he'd have liked face tickles as much as Annie did if he just gave them a chance. I wanted him to know he did have a real friend.

A golden friend!

I wanted to follow Jackson right through the sliding doors at the end of the gallery, but Rex tugged on my tail.

"I know we should chase Jackson again, Sunny. But can't we just stay and look around for a little while?" he asked.

I knew the reason he wanted to stay. At the end of the gallery wall were portraits of all the royal dogs!

I shook my head, as if to say, *No, we can't stay*. But then I gave in. "Okay!" I barked. "For just a minute."

"Rooooowf!" Rex cheered.

These pictures were fun to look at. The dogs in them looked just like us. There were dachshunds and Dobermans; shepherds and shih tzus. And other beagles, of course! Rex came from a long, distinguished line of royal beagles, some of whom had been in the palace centuries ago. And although I had never met any of them, I bet they were all rambunctious troublemakers just like Rex!

Only one royal goldendoodle had ever lived at the palace, so there was only one goldendoodle on the wall.

Me.

The previous spring, I had posed for a painting near one of the ponds out back. I remembered all the dragonflies and fluffy clouds. The painter had included them in my portrait.

"Hey, Sunny," Rex said, looking at my picture and then back at me. "When is *my* portrait going to be painted?"

"Uh . . ." I stammered, "when you behave?"

Rex giggled. "Okay, I'll try harder. I promise. I want to be a part of this gallery more than anything."

"More than a ton of Snappy Snaps?" I asked.

Rex snickered. "Well . . . *close*."

"We'd better go find our cousin before we miss the start of the party," I said.

We headed for the palace ballroom. I guessed that that was where Jackson would go, too.

The back door to the ballroom was open just a crack. It was hard to see when we first walked in. The lights were dim. After a while, our eyes adjusted. Where was everyone?

The staff had set up the dinner tables a little while earlier.

The crystal chandeliers high up on the ceiling sparkled more brightly than the candles. Of course, those were the crystals we had watched the staff polishing one by one earlier that day.

Tables had been decorated with bouquets of gold and silver and bronze balloons that glistened, too.

Like me!

"Wow," Rex said. He was hypnotized by all the sparkle. For the first time all day, that beagle was speechless.

"Look!" Rex barked softly. "By the wall!"

At the side of the room, the furniture had been rearranged. Instead of a large glass cabinet, I saw a row of carnival games. There was a fortune-telling machine, a strong-man machine, and even a foosball table. The ceilings were decorated with brightly colored lights that glowed and buzzed.

Annie and James had posted signs along the wall.

BALLOON ANIMALS

CARD TRICKS

AMAZING MAZES

This had to be the best party ever planned! I couldn't decide which part of the ballroom looked like the most fun to work on.

Jackson didn't seem as impressed. He strolled around the room looking even less happy than he had looked before.

And he started acting so strangely!

He circled around one table and then another. He went around and around the room like some sort of caged animal.

I saw him kick a folding chair for no reason. When it fell over, he kicked another one, and then another. He knocked over an entire row of chairs and he didn't pick up a single one!

After that, Rex and I watched helplessly as

Jackson began grabbing little tins from each of the long, beautifully set tables. He smashed them all to the floor! So much for the party favors. Now they were destroyed.

But Jackson didn't stop there. He seemed determined to mess up everything that had been set up in the ballroom for his birthday.

He actually ripped one of the handmade signs off the wall! I wanted to bark, *Hey! Annie made that sign for you! What's the matter with you?*

But I kept quiet.

"What an animal," Rex said, which was pretty funny, considering the fact that *we* were the dogs in the room.

"You know what it's like to be a troublemaking dog," I asked Rex. "Why would he do this?"

"Hey." Rex growled low. "I would never ruin a party on purpose!"

"No," I said, "you'd just jump into a birthday cake and ruin *that*."

"*Grrrrrrr!* I told you I was hungry. That's all! I have a nose for treats."

"You have a nose for trouble!" I said, laughing. "I know you don't do stuff on purpose, Rex, but still . . ."

"Grrrrrrr."

I knew what *that* growl meant. Time to wrestle! Rex nuzzled me and I nuzzled back. Before we knew it, we were locked in another moment of doggy wrestling. I swatted at him with my golden paws. He swatted me right back.

We were just playing, but we got a little carried away. The two of us rolled under one of the tables and banged into a chair.

It was loud.

"Hello?"

We panted as quietly as possible, so Jackson wouldn't find us.

"Is someone in here?"

I peered out from under the overhanging tablecloth. I could see Jackson twitching a little bit. He looked almost nervous, like he knew he'd done something wrong. Like he knew someone was in there—watching him.

He quickly left the ballroom.

"Wait!" I yelped, jumping out from under the table. "Aw, we'll never find him now!"

"I have an idea," Rex said, pointing to some crumbs on the ballroom floor. Jackson had grabbed a handful of cheesy crunchies on the way out. He dropped crumbs all the way.

I took a lick at the floor just to confirm the fact of the crumbs. If there was one snack that goldendoodles loved, it was cheesy orange crunchies! I licked my lips and my paws. . . .

The crumbs led to a large door that led out of the ballroom. We nudged the door open and went out to the palace patio. The trail of crumbs continued there.

"Let's get him!" Rex barked.

It was the middle of a hot day. The sun was blinding! The sky was so blue! It felt wonderful to be out there in the garden without our collars or our leashes. I felt so free.

Rex didn't waste a minute. That puppy was off and running.

"Rwoowooworroo!" he howled happily.

But I got his attention back. I understood why he wanted to play right now. I did, too! But as much as I wanted to romp around with the pretty butterflies . . .

We had a big job to do!

Our special guest of honor was headed for the palace grove of fruit trees.

And we needed to stay hot on Jackson's tail.

Chapter 6

Jackson raced past pear trees, past apple trees, and through some bushes, until he came to the large pond at the edge of the palace estate.

The wildflowers were in full bloom. I loved running through the tall grass; it tickled my ears.

Rex couldn't have been happier. Every few feet, he stopped at another plant or poked his nose into the dirt to find worms and bugs.

"Where did Jackson go?" I wondered aloud. The cheesy-crunchies crumb trail was long gone.

"There!" Rex had spotted Jackson wandering up ahead of us in a small clearing.

I liked watching our cousin. Everywhere he

walked, he talked to himself and kicked small rocks around. When he came to the enormous pond on our palace property, he picked up a rock and flung it into the water. At first I thought maybe he was trying to skip stones, but these rocks were too big. They made too loud a thunk in the water.

"Hey," I quietly said, "doesn't Jackson know there are fish in there?"

Rex sniffed at the air. "I don't think Jackson cares if there are fish in there."

"Shhhhh," I whispered. "He stopped. I don't want him to hear us."

"Hey, look!" Rex said. "He's gathering more rocks—bigger rocks."

We watched Jackson lift a very large stone off the ground. This time, he took aim at one of the lily pads in the pond.

"Oh, my!" I cried. "What is he doing?"

"Come here, I said!" Jackson yelled, raising the rock over his head. Thankfully, the stone slipped. It was heavy, so it sank straight down.

Thunk.

"Whew," Rex said. "He didn't throw it! Poor fish!"

"Come over here," Jackson said. "Why are you just sitting there? Even you don't want to be my friend, you warty old thing!"

I wondered who Jackson could possibly have been talking to. Then I saw exactly who. In the center of the pond sat an enormous, mud-covered frog. It perched on a boulder, baking itself in the sun, and then hopped onto a very large lily pad.

The frog must have seen Jackson at the water's edge. It was facing in his direction. The old wart-covered frog even croaked loudly, as if to say, *What's up?* Or maybe what he was really saying was *Get away from my place!*

I thought for sure the frog would have tired of Jackson by now. I wished he would just leap from one lily-pad trampoline to the next and bounce safely to shore.

But the frog just sat there. Like a target.

Jackson threw rocks, and the frog just stared at him.

Then Jackson did something scary. He lifted a bigger rock off the ground. It was the size of his entire hand.

Jackson took aim.

"What's he doing?" I asked aloud.

But we knew *exactly* what Jackson was doing.

The frog *still* didn't budge! Didn't that frog know what was coming?

Whoooosh.

The rock that had been in Jackson's hand soared into the air. It went straight toward the frog—and then landed in the deepest part of the pond with a gurgle.

Rex collapsed onto the ground and let out one of his whimpers.

"I thought that frog was . . ."

I made a chopping motion at my neck. "*Toad*ally gone," I quipped.

"Hey!" Rex said. "It's not funny."

Jackson whirled around as if he had heard something. Had he?

Rex got close to me. He was shaking. "You don't think he'd throw big rocks . . . over here? Do you?"

"Who is there? SOMEBODY IS THERE!" Jackson yelled. "COME OUT, BIRD!"

Bird?

He thought we were birds?

Rex and I took deeper cover under a large bush. Unfortunately it was bristly. I nipped at the bristles to get them off my fur.

"You really need to know when to be quiet," I reminded Rex.

"That poor frog is still out there," Rex said, almost whimpering.

"Dumb frog! Dumb birds!" Jackson yelled loudly at the pond. He turned his face to the sky and the trees. "Well, I don't want to be your friend, either!"

I scratched my side with my hind leg. "Who was he talking to? What was he talking about?"

Hold on. Was Jackson *crying*?

I watched as he threw himself on the ground and buried his face in his hands. This was no ordinary temper tantrum.

Jackson was really sad.

Rex and I just looked at each other. We couldn't believe it. Then we realized that Jackson was still holding on to something. . . .

Thwack!

He hurled another rock. This one landed just a few feet away from us.

"Let's go back to the palace," Rex said.

"No, let's *run* back to the palace," I said.

We didn't stick around another moment to see what happened to the frog or the bird or anything else near the pond. We ran through the grass, past all the fruit trees, and back onto the patio.

And slowpoke Rex didn't stop to look at one flower or bug along the way.

"That was a close call," I said, as we stood in front of the palace.

Rex sighed with relief.

We didn't see Jackson anywhere. He hadn't chased us back here.

"You know what?" Rex said to me, his tail wagging again.

"What?" I said.

"I'm kind of hungry, after all that excitement."

I couldn't help but smile.

"Well, there is a gigantic cake in there. And maybe if we're really good, Annie and James will let us have a piece. . . ."

"You had me at *cake*," Rex said. And without another word, he bounded away from me.

I bounded after him, right into the ballroom!

Chapter 7

"Oh, no-o-o-o-o!" I heard someone shout from behind the ballroom doors.

Annie had found the mess that had been left in the ballroom! Rex and I scooted into the room behind her.

"Oh, dear. This is just too much. . . ." Annie said, clinging to the frame of the ballroom door. "Jackson is going to have a fit when he sees this!"

But the room was in worse condition than I'd remembered. There were overturned cups and plates. Two posters on the wall were torn. There were broken party favors everywhere. They'd been stomped into pieces.

"Who would do this?" Annie asked.

Rex and I went over to her. I wanted so much to tell her the truth!

"So there you are, naughty puppies!" Annie cried. "Did *you* do this?"

How could she accuse *us* of making the big mess?

By now, James had come inside the ballroom, too. A look of total shock spread over his face. "What happened here?"

Annie looked as if she were about to cry. "Everything is ruined!"

"Is there something you want to tell us?" James asked his puppy. "Were you in the ballroom today, Rex?"

Rex started to back away. He might as well have just screamed, *I'm guilty! I was here!*

"*You* did all this?" Annie asked. "I told you, James. Your Rex likes to find trouble."

"*Hooooowowooworrroo!*" Rex wailed. He shook his head. "I did not do this! I did not do this!"

I wanted to say, *Hey, don't blame the beagle. He didn't do this.*

Instead, I came up close to Annie and got her attention by brushing my fur against her leg.

"Woof," I barked softly. I was hoping she'd scratch behind my ears.

"Hmm. You don't look like messy pups. There's nothing in your teeth or stuck to your fur. You really didn't have anything to do with this, Sunny?" Annie asked me. "Really?"

I shook my head. I hadn't known if she'd be able to understand, but she did. She understood everything I was saying. She knew I hadn't made the mess.

Annie sat down in one of the chairs and put her head in her hands. This time she really was crying.

"There's only a short amount of time before the guests get here," James said.

"I know! So what are we going to do?" Annie asked.

"Maybe we can clean up in time for the party," James suggested. "The palace puppies can help."

Hey! I wanted to bark out loud. *Why do we have to do all the hard work when birthday boy Jackson is the one who* made *all the mess? He ruined his own party!*

"You really think the puppies can help?" Annie asked, sniffling a little.

I rubbed up against her.

Rex was giving me funny looks from across the ballroom. He had stopped messing with the streamers that had come undone from the wall.

For a moment, I thought he had turned into a mature puppy. We would both help James and Annie to pick up.

And then he flopped onto his back and began rolling around in the paper confetti on the ballroom floor! Oh, Rex! When would he ever learn?

Even if I didn't approve of Jackson's behavior, I needed to be there for Annie and James. This party had to happen, no matter what.

"Rrrrrrroooo!" I shook my head and got Annie's attention back. Then I picked some torn streamers up with my teeth. I trotted over to the garbage can in the corner of the room.

"Sunny!" Annie cried. "What are you doing?"

I showed her exactly what I was doing. I was picking up!

"Aw, Sunny, I should have known you'd do the right thing."

Rex finally joined in next to me. He grabbed a streamer between his teeth, and he walked to the trash can, too. Finally, that puppy was following my lead! Maybe he'd been paying attention all along?

I was proud of him—and of myself.

James let out a *"Whoo-hoo!"* Rex was being a good dog? This was an event!

Even after most of the room had been cleaned up, Annie continued to worry about the mess. The party guests were to arrive soon now. That was a lot of pressure. The prince and princess wanted it to be just right. They wanted Jackson to have a good time.

Annie, James, Rex, and I began to pick up the rest. We turned the royal ballroom into a room fit for a king once again! The staff reset the tables and collected and threw away whatever wasn't needed. One of the palace staff wiped down all the carnival machines.

I sat back on my hind paws, beaming. For the first time in a long time, I felt like a royal pooch. I was ready to be regal again—and not go snooping around the palace. I knew how to behave.

That is—until the birthday cake walked in.

Well, the cake didn't *walk*, exactly. It was carried. But it was the same cake we'd seen hours before in the kitchen, with that same blue frosting.

Mmmmmmmm.

I began to lick my lips uncontrollably.

"Sunny!" Annie said to me. "You're drooling on the floor! What am I going to do with you?"

I scooted backward and tried to stop drooling. But cake is cake. And until I got some, I was a fool for *drool*.

Rex stood off to the side, snickering.

That dog!

I shot him a look, but it was too late. We were dogs! One glance at that sugary sweet concoction, and mischief began to blaze in Rex's eyes. With a charge, he leaped toward the cake.

The table shook as if it had been hit by a tank. Everything wobbled. Rex bounced right off and landed on all four paws. Then he got ready to jump up again.

The second time he leaped up, he made contact. The tip of his snout touched the frosting.

He sniffed hard.

"*Mmmmm*, vanilla," Rex said with a grin, licking his own nose.

"*Step away from the cake, Rex!*" a voice boomed from the other side of the room.

James's whole face had turned red.

"I can't believe you'd jump on Jackson's birthday cake! Bad dog!"

Rex's ears went back again. *Embarrassed.* He stuck his entire head under a cushion on the hall chair.

"Rex!" I cried. "Focus! We need to help Annie and James."

Across the room, Annie and James spoke calmly with other members of the staff. Thanks to our pastry chef's expert skills, they were able to smooth over the part of the frosting that had been nudged by Rex's snout. Everything looked as good as new. The cake was safe at last.

Another one of the chefs came in and put the cake into a large display area. All the palace party guests could admire it from there—before devouring it later.

"Where do you think Jackson went after we saw him in the garden?" Rex asked.

My ears flopped down. I thought about that poor frog.

"You don't feel bad for Jackson, do you?" Rex cried.

"Well," I said thoughtfully, "I know Jackson was throwing rocks at anything that moved, but he seemed so sad and lonely. He's still our cousin, Rex."

"Our rock-throwing cousin," said Rex with a snarl.

All at once, Annie scooped me up into her arms.

James grabbed Rex at the same time.

"Okay, you two troublesome pups," Annie said. "Time to go. The clock is ticking."

My heart sank.

Time to go? Now what?

After all that time helping out, after all that honesty, Rex and I were still going to end up spending a day with Nanny Fran?

It just didn't seem fair.

Chapter 8

Annie squeezed me tightly. I couldn't even squiggle.

How could we have blown our chances to behave? To make matters worse, we'd lost track of Jackson altogether.

Would the princess and prince give us a second chance?

It was hard to live with the idea that I'd never, ever taste a piece of that blue-frosted, delicious cake.

Oh, I should have listened when I had the chance.

"Upstairs . . ." Annie said, a little bit louder. She gave me a kiss on the ear. "We have things to do."

Things to do?

I wanted to whimper again, since it worked so well, or push my way out of Annie's arms and scamper away. I didn't want to miss the party.

Of course, Rex felt the same way as I did, for sure. He wriggled as hard as he could to get out of James's arms. I saw his tail flapping.

"We just wanted to help out!" Rex wailed.

Then all at once, Rex pulled free of James's grip. He jumped into the air and crashed to the floor.

"BOW-WOWWWWWW!" Rex let out a megaphone bark and scooted toward the stairs.

"Rex!" James yelled, chasing him. "Quit messing around!"

But Rex dashed away from his prince.

"Oh, dear!" Annie cried, letting go of me, too. I ran after Rex. "Stop! You palace pups are driving me crazy! No more jumping! We all have to get ready for the party! Stop these shenanigans!"

I didn't know what "shenanigans" were, but I stopped. Had Annie just said *party*?

Rex stopped, too.

We all had to get ready for the party?

"Look, pups, you're members of this royal family, too," Annie said sweetly. "In all the excitement, James and I forgot to get you two ready for the party!"

I nodded my golden head.

She smiled warmly. "Good dog."

Oh, I loved that word: *good*.

"Rex!" I cried. "The princess loves me!"

James snuggled Rex and kissed the top of his head.

"The prince loves me!" Rex woofed.

"Let's get changed! It's getting very late!" Annie said. Then she leaned in to me and whispered, "When we get upstairs, I need to fluff your golden coat and give you some pampering before the others arrive. Is that okay?"

Okay?

I felt like I'd won the lottery!

Rex looked at me and batted his beagle eyelashes in disbelief. If I could have managed a high paw tap, I would have given him one from across the room. His tongue flopped out as he panted with excitement. Jackson wasn't the only one in the castle who was longing for attention.

"ROOOOOOOOOWF!" Rex exclaimed.

"WWWWWOOOOOOOOF!" I yelped back.

"Puppies at the party!" James yelled, pumping his fist.

Annie laughed out loud. "Let's hurry up!"

Never in my wildest doggy dreams would I have imagined that we'd get a real invitation to this party after the way this day had gone.

But here we were, the four of us, skipping upstairs together to get all dressed up!

At the top landing, Rex and James turned left and Annie and I turned right. I raced into Annie's room, jumped onto Annie's bed, and crash-landed on the pile of discarded outfits from the morning.

By now, warm sun had filled the entire room. I rolled my body across the carpet to soak up some of that warmth. Would Annie come over and tickle my tummy?

"Sunny!" Annie cried. "Let's go!"

Oh, well, I thought. The no-tickling thing hadn't changed from earlier that day. But that was okay. There were important things to do.

I got back on my feet and stretched my head up into the air.

Downstairs, the doorbell rang. A clock chimed. *"Children!"* a voice called from below. "The Westerfields have arrived. And I see the Montrose limousine coming after that. . . ."

The queen sounded anxious. The party guests were arriving. We had to hurry to help the queen greet everyone.

Annie flew into a small panic. "Oh, my!" she said as she grabbed the dress she'd chosen that morning and pulled it over her head.

Rrrrrrrrrip!

"No!" Annie cried when she realized what she'd done.

I went over to her and nudged her ever so softly, as if to say, *Calm down, it's just a dress. And the party will be fine. You'll look perfect in whatever you wear. Get another outfit, and let's go!*

I went back to the pile of discarded clothes on the bed and grabbed the green jacket with the buttons. I resisted the urge to chew this time. Instead, I nudged it toward my princess.

"What is *that*?" she asked as she frantically grabbed the jacket from me. "Aw, Sunny . . . You picked this out for me to wear?"

I pushed my snout into the jacket again. *Come on! Try it on!*

She smiled wide. "You like this color on me?" she asked, buttoning those silver buttons.

I wagged my tail.

She sat down on the bed. I couldn't tell if she was about to cry. But then the corners of her mouth curved into the shape of a *U*. "You're such a good dog," she said. "You're my best friend in the whole palace. In the whole world!"

I wagged my tail so hard I almost knocked myself over.

"Woof! Woof! Woof!"

I went over to the dresser and picked up the doggy brush.

Annie took it from me and began to comb my coat.

The brush tickled and I squirmed. How funny! This was a lot like when Annie played with me! She had time for tickles after all!

When I'd been groomed, Annie took out a small gold ribbon and tied some of my fur up into a simple bow atop my head.

Ding-dong.

Bzzzzzz.

Bong! Bong! Bong!

"More guests? We have to go!" Annie said as she rushed to do her own hair. She puffed it up with some hair spray and placed her tiara on top.

Quickly, Annie zipped up the side of her flowered party dress. It had tiny red, orange, and green flowers on it, to match the jacket that *I'd* chosen. In the center of the dress was a silk bow. She looked like such a princess!

Annie applied lip gloss. I knew it was strawberry-milk-shake flavor. It smelled just like a real shake.

"I'm ready to party; you're ready to party. . . ." Annie said. "I just hope Jackson is ready to party!"

I wondered if Jackson was ever ready to party.

And where was he right now, anyway?

On the way out of Annie's and my room, we bumped into James and Rex in the hallway. It reminded me a little of the morning, when I'd nearly collided with Rex out there. So much had happened today—and there was still so much to come!

Rex had on a little doggy sweater emblazoned with the royal crest.

"Nice sweater," I giggled. "You're a very royal palace pup."

Rex poked his nose up into the air. "Like you would expect anything else?"

Paw by paw, we walked down the wide staircase together.

The balustrade still gleamed.

Our coats glistened, too.

We really looked like the perfect palace puppies.

And the long-awaited party was finally about to begin.

Chapter 9

By the time I reached the downstairs landing, my little puppy heart was pounding.

After our great adventure today, I couldn't believe everything had come together so nicely.

The palace seemed like a totally different place.

Party guests were everywhere, mingling in hallways and corridors. Some gazed at paintings on the walls and ceiling. Others looked out at the flower gardens. I hoped that somewhere nearby, Jackson was smiling and enjoying himself, too.

Annie and James had gone to look for him.

The palace staff passed around little hot dogs and rice balls on engraved silver trays. I knew what food was being served, because I could see some appetizer crumbs on the floor.

Rex didn't miss a thing. He poked his nose in and around people's ankles.

"Those little brown things are yummy," he told me. "They taste like our beefy sticks."

I sniffed around for my own treats. Whatever the chicken on a leaf was, I liked it. I liked the red triangles with cheese, too.

"You were right about what you said," Rex said, his nose going fast over the carpet. "People drop a lot! This is fun!"

"*Mmmmmm*, you said it!"

I glanced around the room. Other than the food scraps, tall heels with sparkles on the side, and a bunch of other shoes, I couldn't see much of anything down here. All I knew was that this place was packed!

Jackson sure had a lot of party guests for someone who seemed to be so alone all the time.

When the crowd thinned, I finally got a good look at the decorations that filled the room.

Oh! It looked magnificent. Wide-open windows gleamed as sunlight poured through. Overstuffed pillows filled every chair. Long antique

tables were stacked with silver dishes of candy. Framed landscape paintings lined the walls, and an enormous silver treasure chest sat in the middle of everything. Carved into the sides of the chest were the family names. I spotted Annie's, James's, *and* Jackson's names engraved there.

I kept searching for *Sunny*, but I didn't see it.

Because it was a carnival, a fortune-teller had set up her table in the open foyer to greet and welcome the guests as they arrived. Side tables in the room were crowded with big bowls of fresh flowers. Classical music played over the loudspeakers, too.

Or was that an actual string quartet in the next room?

"Did Annie and James find Jackson yet?" Rex asked me.

I shook my head. "I don't see him anywhere."

"Maybe he ran away," Rex said sadly. "He was so upset the last time we saw him."

"Imagine running away from your own party!" I said.

"Who would do that?" Rex moaned. "Wouldn't he want all his presents?"

"But it's not just about presents," I said. "Doesn't he know how many people here showed up to celebrate with him? Doesn't he care?"

"Let's go look for him again," Rex suggested. "Maybe he found some more rocks to throw. . . ."

"I hope we don't have to walk all over the palace again. . . ." I said with a big sigh. My paws were tired.

But we didn't have to look very far to find the guest of honor.

Jackson was only a few yards away, seated in an enormous, upholstered chair in the center of the room. He sat there as if he were holding court.

I guess that's what royal pains do best.

"Where are my presents?" Jackson asked one of the staff.

The butler didn't know.

"I want my presents!" Jackson said.

"See?" Rex nudged me.

Annie and James came over. "There you are!" Annie said.

"This is my party, and I want to do what I want to do!" Jackson said to them both. "You didn't even finish the setup on time. You left me all alone today, and now you won't give me what I want!"

What a brat! I thought. I wished that boy would be quiet. Annie and James had worked so hard on this party. What was his problem?

"Jackson," Annie said. "There is plenty of food and fun now. And all these people are here to celebrate with you."

"No, they're not here to celebrate with me!" Jackson yelled. He stood up. "No one is even talking to me. Nobody likes me."

Rex looked at me. "No one is talking to him? I wonder why!"

We both snickered. But I couldn't laugh for long. That was too mean, even if Jackson deserved it a little!

I felt sad for Jackson just then. He seemed angry and upset all at the same time. He might have been the guest of honor, but something was very wrong. I didn't want to make fun of him. I wanted to help him.

I padded over to Jackson and nudged his knee with my wet nose.

I heard Annie gasp. "Sunny! Get back here!"

But I didn't go back. I stayed right there, next to Jackson. *Something* was about to happen—I could feel that. Would he kick me? Did he have another rock in his pocket that he might throw at me? Would he yell? Or, would he *like* getting my attention?

"Go away, dog," Jackson moaned.

But I still didn't go. I nudged him again with my wet nose.

"What do you want, you dumb dog?" Jackson yelled.

Annie and James flew across the room when they heard *dumb*.

"Jackson! What did you say to my puppy?" Annie asked.

Jackson crossed his arms across his chest and fell silent.

Everyone stood there, waiting to see what he'd say or do next.

"Jackson?" Annie asked. "What is the matter with you?"

"What's the matter with me?" Jackson wailed louder than I'd ever heard him wail before. "The decorations! The balloons! Everything is the matter!"

"The balloons?" Annie asked. "But they sparkle! I ordered them specially, with my mother's help. You love things that sparkle. Don't you?"

"They don't match anything else," Jackson said. "And balloons are for babies. . . . Oh, why did I ever let you throw my birthday party?"

I nearly jumped out of my doggy fur when I heard that.

How could he say such a terrible thing? How could he think such a horrible thought?

Annie looked as if someone had slapped her across the face. She burst into tears.

"I'm sorry, Jackson!" she cried. "James and I tried our best! We tried our very best!"

"All I wanted was a good birthday party with my friends, but I don't have any friends, and this just proves it!" Now Jackson started to cry.

Just then, the string quartet in the other room started to play.

People began to sing along quietly:

Happy birthday to you!
Happy birthday to you!

I huddled close to Annie's feet. I didn't want her to be sad.

The pastry chef came through the kitchen doors and moved boldly toward the center of the room. The birthday cake looked like a rainbow on a silver platter. It looked even better than it had looked in the kitchen earlier that day, if that was possible.

There was a lot of commotion, so the pastry chef didn't know where to put the cake down. She just stood there for a moment, holding the tray steady.

"Hey," I whispered to Rex.

But he wasn't next to me. And he wasn't in back of me.

Where was Rex?

I looked between legs and around the edges of the chairs and tables. I didn't see him here. I didn't see him there. I didn't see him anywhere!

Happy birthday to yoooooooooooooou!

As the crowd sang the final words, I finally found my partner in crime. Across the room, a few feet away from the chef and the cake, Rex pawed at the carpet like a bull getting ready to charge. He was all worked up.

He was eyeing that cake. Once and for all, he was getting his piece.

Oh, boy, I thought.

Just then, *I* was the fortune-teller at the party. And I predicted disaster.

Rex had already had two near collisions with that cake in the past four hours. And he'd promised James and Annie that he would be good and stay away from it.

But I knew the truth.

Nothing was going to get between Rex and that frosting.

Not even me.

The room exploded in applause for Jackson. He just stood there, looking as unhappy as ever. The chef walked over to Jackson and held the cake up to him for a few photographs. Jackson didn't smile.

Then I saw Rex fly toward the cake, a blur of fur.

Rex and the chef collided with a boom.

The chef lost her balance and tried to keep the cake steady. But in order to stay on her feet, she had to grab something. And what she grabbed was Jackson's vest!

Everyone at the party watched with dismay as the cake flew up off the tray. Rex ricocheted off the servant into Jackson. Jackson crashed to the floor.

Splooooosh.

I watched the layer cake land with a splat right on top of the birthday boy. Rex was still in the air!

He landed on top of Jackson, who was already covered in cake.

The room gasped; then everything went silent.

What would Jackson do? He had been so angry all day long—and now *this*?

But I could not believe what happened next.

"HA-HA-HA!"

Laughter happened next. *Jackson's* laughter.

The birthday boy was covered from head to toe with cake and frosting, but he was *laughing*.

Even his eyes were lit up with happiness.

Rex looked happy, too. With several giant licks, he went to work on the frosting that covered Jackson's head, face, and neck. He began licking the frosting from everywhere.

He'd entered the cake zone.

Quickly, I raced over and began to poke with my nose and paws at Jackson. I licked some frosting off his hand.

"*Rowf?*" I asked; in puppy speak, that meant *Are you okay?*

Jackson looked right at me. His frown had vanished completely. And the more frosting Rex licked, the more loudly Jackson laughed.

His laughter was contagious.

Which meant that soon, *everybody* at the party was doubled over.

Even me.

Chapter 10

Earlier that afternoon, Jackson had been throwing rocks at frogs and sobbing at his own birthday party. Now, he was laughing.

It made me wonder: was Jackson laughing *with* us? Or was this some kind of sinister trick? What if Jackson was about to get even *madder* than before? What if his pockets were filled with rocks right now?

It was hard to trust someone who was always so difficult to understand.

Jackson wiped some of the smeared frosting off his chin and went over to Annie and James.

"Cousins," Jackson said, still smiling, "I have something to tell you."

"Are you all right?" Annie asked. I'm not sure she trusted what was happening, either. But no matter how upset she might have been, Annie always worried about people. This made her a great friend to everyone.

Jackson knew that. He hung his head. "Uhhh…" he mumbled.

The whole room waited for him to speak.

"Uhhh . . ." James interrupted. "Got cake?"

Jackson smiled. "Thanks, Cousin James," he said, "and I got cake. Here, have some. . . ."

Jackson took a scoop of frosting and smeared it onto James's forehead. James cracked up. Then the rest of the room started laughing, too

"Thanks, Annie and James. For the party. I know you guys don't even like me that much. I guess it's okay if I don't have any friends—"

"What? That's not true!" Annie said. "Why would you say that? We like you, Jackson! We're your friends!"

"Yeah," James nodded, "even though you can sure be a royal pain sometimes!"

Jackson smiled. "I guess . . ."

"Look at all these other people here who love you, Jackson." Annie opened her arms and looked around the room. "Everyone here is your friend. But to have *good* friends, you have to *be* a good friend."

"Yeah," Jackson hung his head again. "I know."

"I'm sorry the cake landed on you, Jackson," Annie told him. "The dogs were just excited. . . ."

"Well, maybe I deserved it," Jackson replied.

"Huh?" Annie got a twisted look on her face. "What did you say?"

Jackson looked down at me and Rex. We were covered in blue frosting. We must have been quite a sight!

"I haven't behaved very well today," Jackson said. "Have I?"

"Well," James said, "not really."

The king and queen were walking toward us! I crouched behind Annie's legs. Jackson's parents were there, too.

"Jackson," his mother said, shaking her head, "you behaved terribly today, son! I think you owe everyone an apology."

Jackson nodded. "You are right, Mother. I'm sorry to the king and queen, to Annie and James, to everyone."

Jackson looked down at me and Rex.

"I'm even sorry to you two!" he said.

Annie chuckled. "Why were you so unhappy, anyhow?"

"I just wanted you all to like me," Jackson said.

"So you screamed at us?" James asked. "Yeah, that makes sense."

"No," Jackson explained. "I wanted you to be my friends."

"James is right," Annie said. "Yelling at someone is probably *not* the way to make friends. I guess you know that now."

"Sometimes I just feel lonely," Jackson admitted. "I don't have a brother or a sister or anything."

Everyone got very quiet.

He'd admitted what I'd known all along.

"I'm sorry if I made a mess," Jackson said.

Annie and James stepped forward to give Jackson a hug.

"Wait!" he cried. "I'm still covered in—"

"Frosting?" Annie said, licking her arm, which now had a bunch of the sweet stuff on it.

Jackson laughed. "I guess sometimes I can be a little bit of a pain. I'll try harder, promise."

Jackson scooped a sticky Rex up in his frosting-covered arms.

"Now, let's party!"

In the end, the cake was ruined, but the party was saved. A huge success! The party guests had many carnival activities to choose from. No one had anything to complain about.

There was face-painting and dancing. A juggling troupe gave a demonstration in the ballroom—juggling bowling pins! The royal magician did a rope trick. I wished I could do magic tricks! I joked to Rex that he could do magic. After all, he had made an entire cake disappear.

The queen announced that a second birthday cake would be rushed to the palace. That was how it worked at royal parties. If something broke, someone swooped in and fixed it. Or, in the case of the cake, *frosted* it.

Music started up again in the background, and I started to shake back and forth a little to the beat.

It wasn't the strings this time that got me moving. Annie and James had the royal DJ, London, spin some music.

James shook his hips. London knew all of his favorite songs.

"Being a good friend takes work," Annie explained to Jackson. "You stay loyal and sweet. You can't act mean or spoiled."

"In other words, you can't act like me," Jackson said.

"Exactly," James quipped.

"I'm . . . I'm . . . sorry," Jackson said. "I'm lucky to have friends and family like you."

"Yes, you are!" Annie said. She pointed around the room. Then she pointed right at me and Rex. "And the palace puppies are your good friends, too!"

Annie leaned down and picked me up. I flopped into her arms. I loved every single hug I got. I licked Annie's face to tell her "Thank you."

"Sunny is the best friend a girl could ever have," Annie said. "No one can resist a palace puppy, Jackson. Not even you!"

"Yeah. Rex isn't so bad, either," James said. "He's *my* pal."

Rex growled.

"My *best* pal," James said, correcting himself.

"I'll try better next time to be the best party

guest and a better friend, I promise," Jackson said. "Maybe I can make it up to you both on *your* birthdays?"

"Yes," James said. "I'd like you to get me . . ."

"James!" Annie interrupted. "Stop making lists of things you want. Friendship isn't about presents. Remember?"

"It's not?" Jackson looked a little dejected. "So I guess I won't be getting any gifts this year?"

"SURPRISE!"

A servant appeared with an enormous box. Inside were piles of perfectly wrapped presents. Some had bows, some had cards. Jackson took the box enthusiastically and plopped backward into the chair.

"Presents!" he said. *"Wow! For me?"*

We all watched as he ripped into the pile. He couldn't change from spoiled brat to perfect boy in one afternoon, I thought. But he was off to a good start!

While Jackson opened the gifts, Annie, James, Rex, and I danced around in a little circle. Annie did that doggy tango thing I loved so much. I felt so light on my paws.

No one seemed to mind that they were still

covered with frosting. The royal photographer snapped loads of funny pictures for the palace photo albums. Even the king and queen joined in the festivities.

The guests didn't get party favors, since they'd all been broken earlier in the day, when Jackson stormed the ballroom. But we got that second cake! The servants brought in a giant frosted yellow cake. And so we celebrated with a dessert that was as golden as me. *Delicious!*

"Hold on!" James said as the staff cleared away the cake plates. "There's one present we nearly forgot. It's from your mom and dad."

It was a large box marked SPECIAL DELIVERY, with a card attached that said, *You've Got a Friend.*

Jackson looked confused. "What is this?"

I scratched my side with one paw. What *was* inside that box?

Rex's nose sniffed madly at the air. "I know what's in there!" he said. "Happy! Happy! Happy!"

All at once, the gift box *moved.*

I jumped. We heard a low noise. It was coming from inside the box!

"ROOOOOOOOFF!"

The top of the box flew open.

Puppy?

Inside the box was a cute pug with a squished-up nose and perky little ears. This pug had a stripe of white on its back, too. There were holes in the box, but I hadn't noticed them until the pooch appeared.

Jackson looked dumbfounded. "A puppy? For me?"

The poor pug looked a little scared of all the people in the room. He climbed right back into the box again!

I pulled the box over with my paws and climbed inside. I wanted to tell this pup that everything was okay! Immediately, the pug puppy began to lick frosting off me.

Jackson's face went pink. "Wow," he said. "I don't know what to say."

"Well," Annie teased, "a thank-you would be nice. And then, how about a hello? He's all yours! Hold him up so we can see him!"

Jackson didn't frown a single time after that. He played with his new friend and enjoyed the rest of the party guests, too. Of course, soon it was late and time to head home. The staff brought all of Jackson's gifts to the family limousine, except

for the pug, which Jackson insisted on carrying.

Jackson wasn't about to let go of that present.

"See you soon, Jackson!" Annie called out from the front door of the palace.

"Not if I see you sooner!" Jackson called back. He and the pug waved good night. "Thanks for the party, and thanks for being such great friends."

The king and queen were impressed by all the hard work their children had done for the party. James tried to take most of the credit, of course, and Annie hated it when he did that.

"Um," she said, "I think we *all* worked hard today." She winked at me.

I couldn't believe how quickly the palace staff took down all the decorations and displays that had been put up that morning. In no time, the palace was back to its preparty state.

Soon, Annie and I were back up in her room together, getting ready for bed. Annie gave me a doggy bath with lavender-and-lemon-smelling shampoo, in a separate, smaller doggy tub in her bathroom. It had the royal crest embossed on the side.

After my bath, Annie combed and blow-dried

my fur, too, gently stroking my head. This was the kind of attention I was used to!

"You know," she said to me as she closed the heavy curtains and got the room ready for us to go to sleep, "I am very proud of you, Sunny. I meant what I said about you being the best friend ever. You really *are* my best friend in the world."

I nodded my puppy head. I wanted Annie to know that I understood every word she said. I loved her so much.

"I'm a lucky princess," she said, her voice dragging a little bit.

And Jackson is lucky, too, I wanted to bark, *to have friends like you and James.*

Annie's eyes were getting very heavy. Soon, she'd be fast asleep.

"I'm glad that Jackson got his own puppy today," she said. "We'll have to have a palace playdate very soon."

Slowly, she drifted off to sleep. I watched her breathing and snuggled close. Soon enough, I'd be in doggy dreamland myself. That was a magical place where all good puppies went after a long day at the palace.

Whatever I dreamed, I knew one thing for

sure: there would be lots of friends there to chew bones, play tag, and roll around in the warm sun.

And maybe even some frosted cake to share.

Bow-wow!
Give a royal welcome
to the next book
in the Palace Puppies series:

PALACE
PUPPIES
Sunny to the Rescue

Laura Dower